It's All About The Honeybee

A tale about a beekeeper and his wife

Written by Therese Povolo
Illustrated by Greg Griswold
Edited by Elysha Davila

First edition
Bud and May Publishing 2021
contact: Therese Povolo
tapovolo@gmail.com
Edited by Elysha Davila

ISBN-978-0-578-83264-7

This book is dedicated to our parents,
Patricia and Arthur, and Betty and Raymond

Beatrice and Herman lived in the country with their honeybees and their big garden.
Herman took care of the honeybees, and the honeybees gave him lots of honey.

Herman loved his honeybees and even acted like them. He acted like them so often that it caused Beatrice to wonder about Herman. She imagined him turning into a honeybee. She was pretty sure that could never happen.

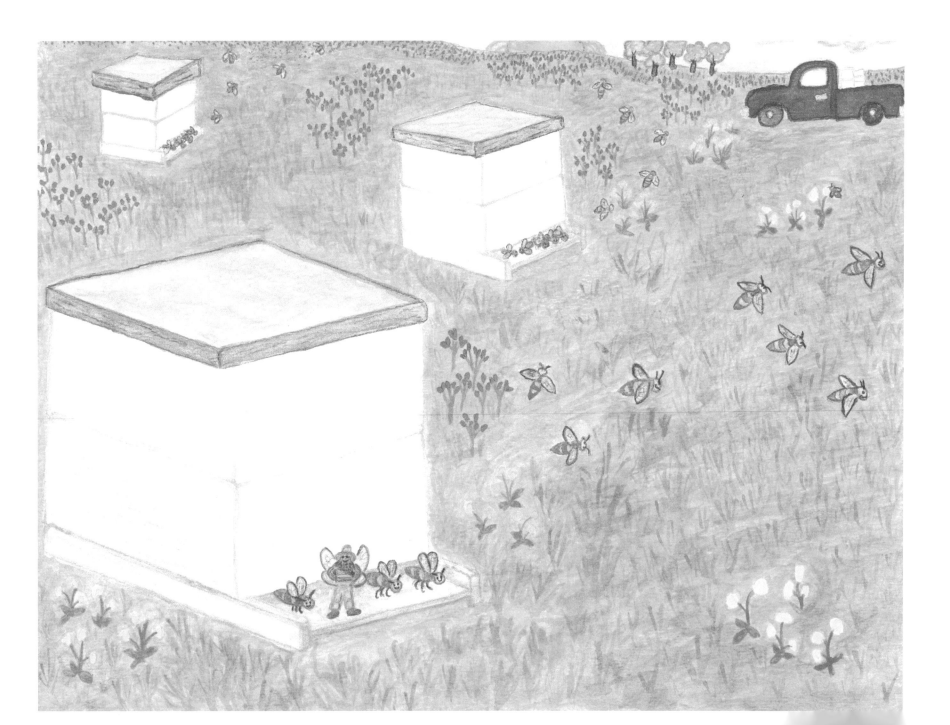

Like his honeybees, Herman loved honey.
He ate it in his oatmeal at breakfast.
He ate it for lunch in his peanut butter sandwiches.
He ate fresh honeycomb all day long while he
hung out with his honeybees.

Herman dressed like a honeybee.
He had pockets on his pants that
stored everything he collected all
day just like the pollen sacs on his
honeybees.

Bees collect pollen from flowers and bring it back
to their hives to feed the babies.
They also collect nectar from flowers. They bring
nectar back to the hive and turn it into honey.

Rain is good for flowers, and honeybees need flowers; but honeybees don't go out flying in the rain. Herman stayed in when it rained too.

Herman buzzed like his bees. Honeybees buzz to tell each other important things. Herman buzzed with them on his kazoo.

Honeybees dance for each other, they do a waggle dance to show each other the map to the flowers.

Herman danced with Beatrice every morning while he circled and spun and buzzed his way out the door.

So that is why Beatrice wondered about Herman turning into a honeybee. One day, while she was at the farmers market selling honey, it was all she could think about.

One night it kept her
awake all night long.

The next day Herman and Beatrice took a drive. Herman was jumping in his seat happy about all the wild flowers blooming. Fields and shrubs and trees were covered in flowers filled with nectar that would make delicious honey.

Beatrice decided to tell Herman her thoughts about him turning into a bee.

Herman smiled and said, "Well if I can become a honeybee, you can become one too!"

"We will fly among the flowers, sucking up nectar and gathering pollen; and bring it back to our hive."

Beatrice liked the idea of being able to fly, but then she said, "Herman you can't turn into a honeybee because the bees need you to be their beekeeper! You keep them safe from pests, and you keep them from getting sick. The farmers that grow our food need the bees."

Herman said, "You are right, beekeepers take care of the bees, and the bees take care of us humans. I only act like the bees to understand them better since honeybees are so special, and so important."

So, while Herman remained a beekeeper who acted like his honeybees, Beatrice found a way that they could fly together.

Authors note: "To know bees, is to love bees" is the motto of Champion Hill Farm, the beekeeping business which Greg Griswold and I own and operate. Greg, who has been keeping bees since 1984, works towards the mission of managing our hives with individual care, respect and attention.

To Know Bees, is to Love Bees!

Champion Hill Farm
Beulah, Michigan

Acknowledgement
We would like to thank all our landowners, both past and present who have made space on their properties to host our honeybee hives. Your dedication to sustainable agriculture and respect for nature are paramount to the survival of the honeybee.